COSMOGLYPH

COSMOGLYPH

John Paine

ATHENA PRESS
LONDON

ISBN 978 1 84748 700 1

First published 2010 by
ATHENA PRESS
Queen's House, 2 Holly Road
Twickenham TW1 4EG
United Kingdom

Printed for Athena Press

To Bet, Joan, Chris and my beloved Alexandrina

My thanks to Steven and to Spirit

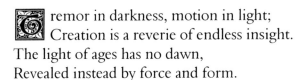remor in darkness, motion in light;
Creation is a reverie of endless insight.
The light of ages has no dawn,
Revealed instead by force and form.

What I am is what I am not.
Conceived of my sources, in circles of art,
Ringed together, loops of divinity –
A cosmic riddle expressed as infinity.

Sinking through clouds of nebular dust,
Galactic clusters swirl and thrust,
Interstellar whirlpools, whose irradiation
Sprayed spatial voids with dancing atoms.

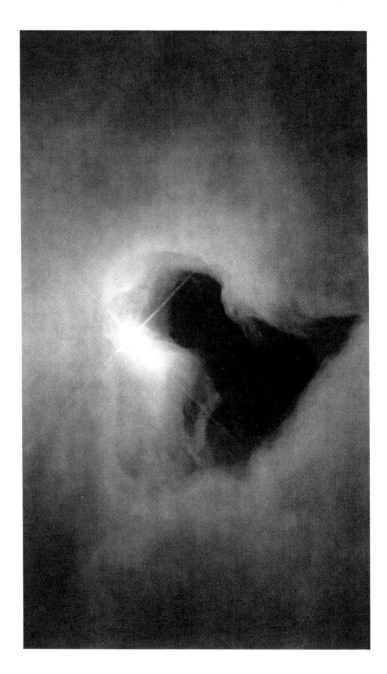

he solar system divided by a process;
Pulsaric witness to an awesome
  mitosis.
Vast haloes of gaseous activity,
Accompanied each celestial nativity.

Corpuscles of fire and heavenly light
Ricocheted out at the cosmic night.
Sparks impressed with a cause divine,
Subjugate matter, overtake time.

Scientists now say we are empty space;
Wherein do we behold the human race?

Atomic structure is not the heart
Of all that lies in light and dark.
The straightest line, now curved, can throw
More light than any comet's glow.

Aries

rion's Belt and the Great Bear
Were born of coruscating flares.
A million suns began to dawn
Before the Milky Way was spawned.

The Lords of Flame and Form and Mind,
Great Regents of the astral kind,
Forged the spheres and stars in chains,
To grace the embryonic plains.

The Milky Way, an Empyrean,
A pendant of stars and solar dreams.
In the darkest recess of planetary space,
Devouring Saturn showed his face.

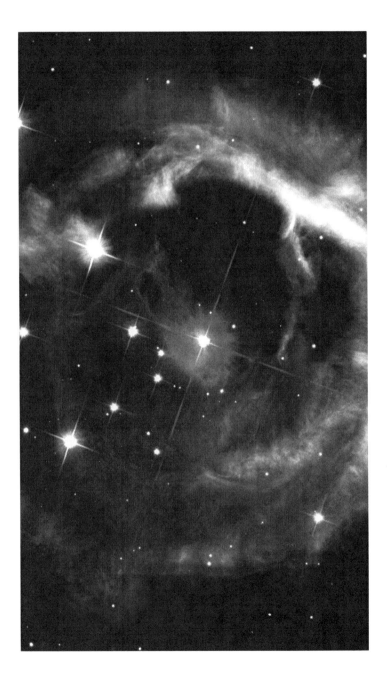

aturn burned so clear and bright
For countless aeons – a titan ringed in
   light –
Scythed warrior of our family spheres,
While the Sun King grew his beard.

All the planets from fragmentation,
Fissiparous medium of nuclear fission.
The life of all in the life of one,
From craterous Moon to perfect Sun.

Venus, midwife of the Earth,
Brought her from the fiery birth,
From cataclysmic fire and flood;
Auriel's mantle staunched the blood.

Pisces

The Earth spun wildly and split in two,
Its lunar twin had the stronger pull.
Amid meteor showers and Hadean terrain,
Gaia's bequest to kin Promethean.

As planetary forces began to develop,
Now stresses and influences each to their
  level:
Saturn to origins, then to restriction,
Jupiter to growth and spiritual conviction,
Venus to beauty and natural abstraction,
Mars to emotion and infatuation,
Mercury to mind and mental conviction,
The Moon, a force of etheric projection,
Earth to dense matter and incarnation.
The Sun to spiritual inspiration,
Alchemical fire and regeneration
Of soul and final transmutation.

ife swarms past great cosmic phases,
Schooled in sojourns through the
  arcane nebulae.
From Taurus's eye they first streamed down,
Scattered on the earthly ground.

The spirit of God said, 'Let there be light.'
Did She really have in mind the lowly sight
Of an algal pool of floating debris?
Scarcely the blueprint for a horse or tree!

The life of all is in the unicellular –
From microbe to the Crab Nebular.
Each orb a universal power,
Each cosmic seed a human flower.

Capricorn

zekiel envisioned the four Holy
quarters –
Lion, Ox, Eagle and Centaur –
Each a grail of divine grace,
The great harbingers of Adam's race.

When man first crouched upon burning
    plains,
His body one with sentient brain,
His life was short, his instincts strong:
An earthen child from star line long.

The creative spark behind the body
Contacted gamma in Alpha Centauri.
A stellar blueprint, a revolution
Of powers, of matter and spirit in fusion.

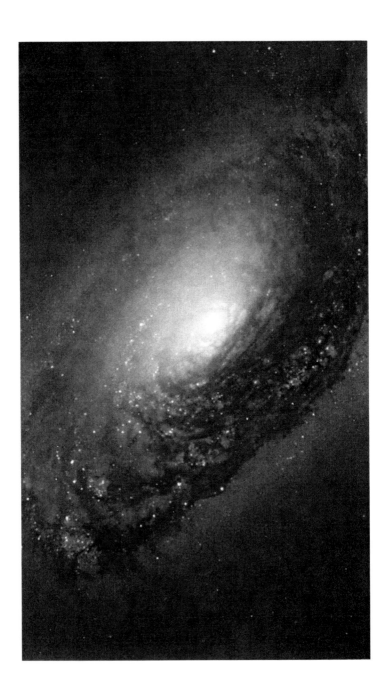

he Lemurians were gentle, peaceful and meek,
Their souls were immense, though their
    bodies were weak.
They considered their race part of one
    cosmic whole
And declined to accept a mere mortal role.
Man is more than flesh and blood,
He is thoughts and feelings in a transient
    mood –
A dreamer, cosmographer, adventurer,
    redeemer,
Poet, reciter, mystic and creator.
Reconcilers of passion with inner wisdom,
Serene in the harmony of equilibrium.

Aquarius

he governing ethos of this civilisation:
Sagacity, humility and toleration.
From cities on the plains to wooden erection,
Through gardens of Babylonian projection.
In shaded vistas, along gentle declivities,
Marble-crested pantheons and municipalities.
Some called this time the Garden of Eden.

The fall into matter and degeneration
Was really a question of sensory perception.
Man came to believe only senses were real;
He lost all thought of life's great wheel.

he Lemurians were an intuitive race,
They telepathised into a distant space.
Contacts were made with the system Arcturus
And psychic awareness was channelled to
  Sirius.
Truth, as the ancient Druids would tell,
Found only in the silence of the deepest well.

A mighty explosion smashed Gaia's haven,
As asteroid fragments impacted in flame.
Thousands perished as the Earth spun wild,
Formed palls of smoke – a primal shroud.

Sagittarius

Survivors of this gentle race
Founded Atlantis in another place,
A continent larger than Australasia,
A haven of shelter and hidden favour.

Atlanteans worshipped the heavenly sights –
Progress of Mars, Saturn's transit.
Their stellar wisdom and magical rites
Promoted healing, technology and cosmic
   insight.

A Temple of the Moon was their greatest
   treasure,
Diana's remains held within her.
Atlanteans needed no tablets of stone;
The Moon, their mistress, helped them atone.

S ea life – both concise and brutal –
Hunters, scavengers and cannibals,
Under copper sun and lapis sky,
The wicker men would fight and die.

Merlin, high priest of the starry wisdom,
Sailed to Ireland to avoid destruction.
The Celts saw him as a sage magician,
Refugee of a mystery Avalonian.

Later, Atlantis declined as a culture,
Man's nature becoming akin to the vulture's,
Planetary despoilers on a mission hell-bent,
Picking away the carcass with clinical intent.

Scorpio

he Lord Auriel warned of the deluge to come,
In visions and dreams only granted to some.
Noah's ark was the legend of biblical fame;
In reality, survival was more than a game.

Thousands perished when the cataclysms came,
Five of them smashed the Atlantean plains.
Volcanic upheavals and Earth's orbital shift
Produced an acceleration of continental drift.
Tidal waves and earthquakes submerged the continent,
Immersing all but the memory of it.

As Gemini ended, a comet flashed by –
A flaming tribute against the sky.
To man's endeavour, Chaldeans' bane,
Astrology born in a cradle of flame.

Abram of Ur met Melchizedek
To wrest from his mind and intellect
Thoughts and forms and wisdom's might –
A torch to guide to day from night.

Abram retained the hopes of his race,
To lead them on to their rightful place.
Abraham now, Lord of the Sands,
To lead his sons to the Promised Land.

The ladder of Jacob, tier after tier,
Circle on circle, sphere within sphere.
The torment of Joseph turns in on itself,
Within the tormentor, his celestial self.

Libra

he age of Taurus: a time to reflect;
To bring forth stability, left often in
   check;
The time of the shaman and parochial law,
Confucian ideas and philosophical man.

On mist-haunted swords in circles of stone,
The Druids awaited the sun to atone.
With mistletoe, oak and incense of yew,
These shamans transcended the worlds that
   they knew.

Where light and dark are mingled,
Where time itself was born,
Where Pan his pipes blows softly
And Herne his hunting horn.

Mosaic Law inscribed in stone,
Layered steps from God's great throne.
Did Moses truly see the light
Or were the words his own insight?

Zarathustra crouched alone,
Inner doubts his mortal bane.
God's hand he saw, the sun recalled,
Yet had God's love begun to pall?

The sun entered Aries on the ecliptic,
When human nature sought the heroic.
The Greek deified the great and imperfect,
Mythologised man in his celestial aspect.

Virgo

he new, bright age shaped mankind's
Gods –
Olympian Zeus, imperial Jove –
With thunderbolts they held their thrones.
Where are the eagles, red with the warring?
Where are the spears atremble with slaughter?
Spartan armies, Roman legions,
The bannered hosts, the fighting demons –
Carthage fell to their might,
The walls of Troy drowned in waves
Of armoured hosts with bows and glaives.
The dramas of Sophocles, the voyage of
   Odysseus,
The Great Alexander, the triumph of Perseus.

The age of heroes, the age of war,
The rolling dice, the wretched poor –
Trodden down beneath the hooves,
Their bodies scattered, their homes unroofed.

hough armies fought and empires fell,
Gautama, within his cell,
Serenity preached and lasting peace,
To give the world another lease.

A shooting star appeared in space
To light the firmament ablaze.
The alignment of Venus with a supernova
Meant another great age was over.

The ethereal aura of the Moon
Vibrated to distant cosmic tunes.
The greatest flow of light on Earth
Came to bring man second birth.

Leo

The Lord Gabriel shone through the veils of light sleep
To notify mysteries and truths so deep.
The sleeping shepherds, magi and kings
Understood little of heavenly song.

An ordinary mother and earthly father –
Unlikely parents for a human Saviour.
Some called this event the Immaculate
    Conception –
They were victims of an elaborate deception.

Jesus was born an ordinary man,
No immediate exception to the earthly plan.
How could we all have feet of clay,
When he was conceived so naturally?

Jesus was a being not wholly divine,
But a holy soul with a human mind.
He suffered torment in his youth,
From feelings that he was uncouth.

s sons of God, we have the ability
To realise our cosmic destiny.
To Jesus on a mountain top, dancing in the
 light,
God's hawk becomes a dove to make it all
 come right.

Jesus wandered the deserts of Arabia
And studied esoteric truths of every flavour.
His love of knowledge, of nature and people
Unfolded his soul to the ineffable.

The purple ray and the solar power
Started to infiltrate Earth's aura.
They watered this one human flower,
Until it became a resplendent bower.

Cancer

esus believed with great conviction
In a doctrine of love and total freedom;
To live for others and succour many
Was a lifestyle considered revolutionary.

He healed the sick and cleansed the leper,
Through mighty bursts of solar power.
He feared these glimpses of immortality
And yearned to be at peace and just ordinary.

Lazarus's temple was bandaged and foul,
When he stumbled in the light to the
    Pharisees' scowl.
He shed his death and sat down beside his
    Lord
To commune with Love on the power of the
    Word.

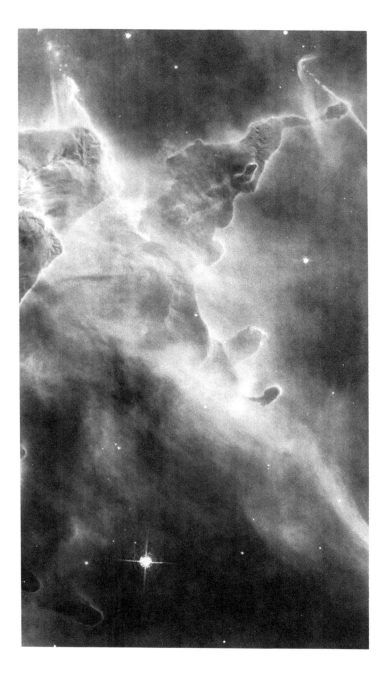

ust behind every city gate
Await coteries of fundamentalist hate –
Those who questioned his right to speak
Still seek to place him out of reach.

Jesus did not want to be divine,
Just to have a chance to be kind
And for others to share his dream
Of peace on Earth.

Why did people think it strange
That all his friends ran away,
That all his hopes went astray,
That only his fears had remained,
That all expectation had decayed,
That the only person he refused to save was
Himself?

Gemini

he man from Galilee winced in pain
As pieces of whalebone split his skin.
A splintered crossbeam pressed down his
   head,
His heart was filled with fear and dread.
Pain and loathing filled his soul
For what he had to undergo.
Was it no one's fault but his own,
All because they wouldn't leave him alone?

The revenge of the moneylenders was
   complete;
As they hammered his wrists and impaled
   his feet,
Agony twisted every nerve.
To die like a criminal seemed absurd.

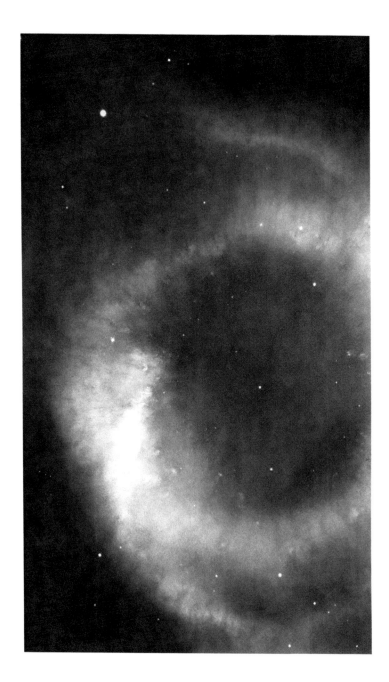

Jesus felt himself a failure –
No great faith, nor earthly Saviour.
A symbol of local veneration
Became one of universal execration.

The riddle of the missing body was unfair
And rather akin to Burke and Hare.
What he had promised to exhibit
Was not to rise in flesh, but spirit.

The Church he founded was man-made,
It exploited Jesus from the grave.
His death became the great sacrifice –
A useful liturgical device.

Taurus

he early Church's philosophy
Was fashioned on an obedience to
  authority;
Belief in reincarnation and personal salvation
Were soon consigned to oblivion.

Throughout its first millennium,
The Church built itself on fear and repression,
Torture, execution, acquisition and greed
Were principal tenets of the creed.

From the Crusades to Schism, Reformation
  to Inquisition,
The churches, militant, starved and
  imprisoned.
The suffering, fear, guilt and shame
Meant they were crucifying their master again.

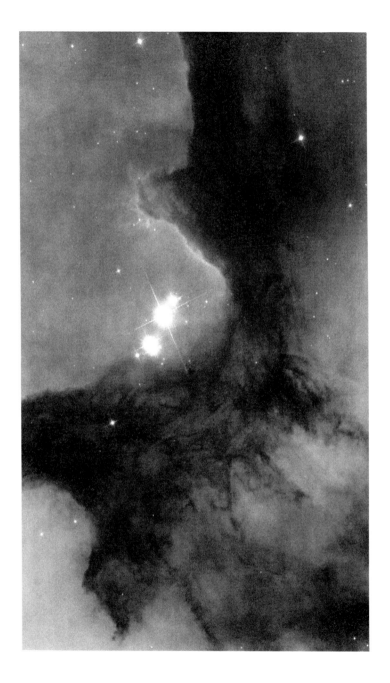

The precession of the equinoxes,
The movement of the sun in eclipse,
A shift of the universal zodiac
Soon inaugurates the Age of Aquarius.

Cataclysms will soon shake the Earth,
As continents subside and shift.
Societies will divide and rift,
Compassion will become the greatest gift.

Healing, telepathy and meditation
Will become the planetary inspiration.
A growing awareness of the inner self
Will launch man from his cosmic shelf.

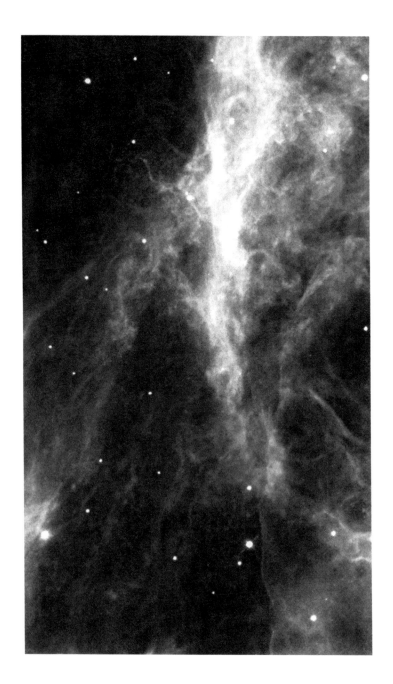

An end to war and greed and pain
Are not such unrealistic aims.
To deliver the fruits of a higher mind
May reconcile us to love divine.

~ END ~

Lightning Source UK Ltd.
Milton Keynes UK
19 March 2010
151572UK00001B/36/P